MARGRET & H.A. REY'S
Curious George
and the Pizza Party

Written by Cynthia Platt

Illustrated in the style of H. A. Rey by Mary O'Keefe Young

HOUGHTON MIFFLIN HARCOURT
Boston   New York

For Charlotte & Caroline, who love pizza pie
—C.P.

For my brilliant Autumn
—M.O'K.Y.

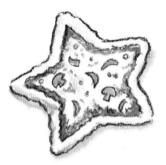

The text of this book is set in Adobe Garamond.

The illustrations are watercolor.

Library of Congress Cataloging-in-Publication Data is on file.

ISBN 978-0-544-10988-9

Printed in China

SCP 10 9 8 7 6 5 4 3 2 1

4500423124

George was a good little monkey and always very curious. Today, he wasn't just curious—he was excited. So excited, in fact, that he was turning flips and standing on his head!

A little girl in George's building had invited him to her pizza party. George had never been to a pizza party before, but he loved parties and he loved pizza, so he knew it had to be good.

"George, it's time for the pizza party," said the man with the yellow hat.

"Have fun—and remember to be on your best behavior!"

George got to the party in perfect time!

"Hi, George," called out the little girl. But oh, what was all of this? The children were wearing puffy white chef's hats and checkered aprons.

George got a hat and an apron, too! The best was yet to come.
They weren't just going to eat pizza. They were going to make
it, too.

"Everyone will get a piece of pizza dough to roll out and make
a special pizza," explained the girl's mother. There were many
little lumps of dough.

"But first, let's play some games!" she said.

Everyone went into the living room to play pin the pepperoni on the pizza. Everyone, that is, except George. He was curious about those pieces of dough.

   George thought and thought. If lots of little pieces of dough were good, maybe one huge one would be even better.

He gathered the lumps of dough together and squished and squashed them until they became the very biggest piece of dough he'd ever seen. What fun! Maybe rolling it out would be even more fun!

George poured flour out on the table, and he rolled and rolled and rolled the dough with a rolling pin.

It was messy work! First he bumped over one of the chairs.

Crash!

Then he knocked over the sack of flour. *Thump!*

The flour looked like snow lying on the floor of the kitchen.
George liked snow, though, so he didn't mind at all.
Soon he had gotten the dough nice and thin.

But the thinner it got, the farther it spread out.
Before he knew it, the dough covered the
table . . . then the chairs . . . and then George.

Without the flour, it started to stick to everything—including George!
George stopped to think.
  Maybe the dough was better off in small pieces after all.

George got a pair of scissors and began cutting
up the dough into lots of different shapes.
He thought everyone would be pleased.

"George! What have you done to the kitchen?"
The little girl's mother didn't look very happy.
"I think it's time for you to go home now."
   How surprised and sad George was.

Just then, the children burst into the kitchen and saw the mess that George had made.

"George, what happened?" asked one boy. The other children looked at the shapes George had made with wide eyes.

"Wow, George! I've never seen pizza dough like that before," said the little girl, smiling.

"Well," said her mother, "if you can clean up this mess quickly, George, I suppose you can still stay to make pizza."

The children all helped George clean the kitchen.
He was lucky to have so many good friends.
  As they worked, they talked about the pizza!
 "I'm going to make a pizza that looks like a star," said
one little boy.
  "And I'm going to make one that looks like
a house!" said a girl.

Once the kitchen was clean, the real fun began!
All of the children picked out perfect pieces of
dough and got to work.

They spooned on tomato sauce and sprinkled on cheese.
They added lots of vegetables and pepperoni.

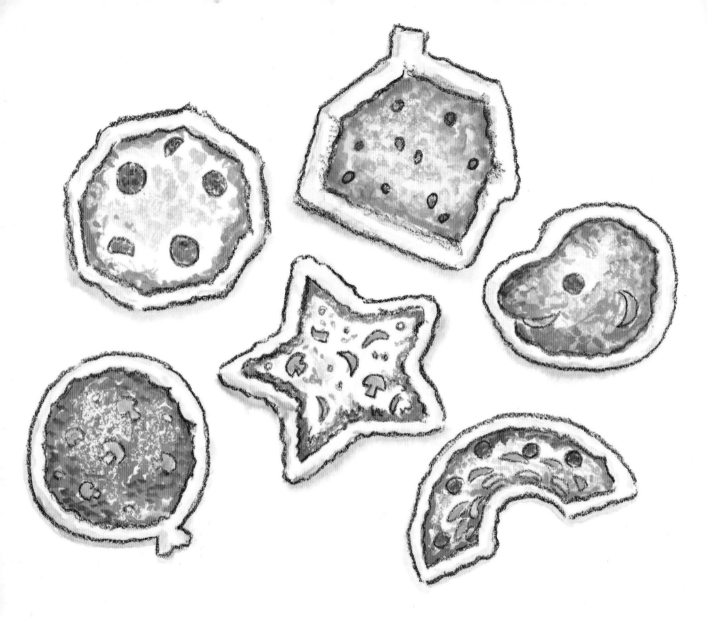

The pizzas looked wonderful! One looked like a rainbow,
another like a stop sign, and still another like a balloon.
There was even a pizza that looked curiously like George!

"Well, George," said the little girl's mother, "the pizzas taste great, and thanks to you, they look wonderful, too!"

Everyone agreed. It was the best pizza anyone had ever seen—or tasted!

For the second time that day, George was so
happy that he turned flips and stood on his head.

Of course, it was a little harder to turn flips with so
much pizza in his belly. But George didn't mind.
It had been a wonderful pizza party!